# HOW DOES YOUR GARDEN GROW?

### By Pat Patterson
### Illustrated by Brenda Clark and Debi Perna

 **An OWL Magazine/Golden Press Book**

Published in Canada by Greey de Pencier Books, Toronto. Canadian Cataloguing in Publication Data Patterson, Pat. How does your garden grow? ISBN 0-920775-02-0 I. Clark, Brenda. II. Perna, Debi. III. Title. PS8581.A77H69 1985   jC813'.54   C85-098290-1   PZ7.P37Ho 1985

An earthworm was crawling along. Suddenly the earth around him started to crack and crumble in a most alarming way.

"Hey! What's going on here?" the earthworm asked himself. He wriggled his long, pink body up through the soil to find out.

No wonder the earth was moving! Someone was digging with a spade. It was a girl. To the earthworm she looked very big.

The earthworm crawled to a safe corner
of the garden. There he was joined by a
caterpillar, an ant, and a snail.

The girl, whose name was Gaily, dug, hoed, and raked. Her little brother, Sebastian, helped her.

This was the first time Gaily had ever made a garden of her very own.

When the earth was ready, Gaily carefully planted some seeds.

"It's raining!" exclaimed the snail.
"I'm going inside my shell to stay dry."
   "Oh, dear," said the caterpillar,
crawling under a leaf at the edge of the
garden. "When my fuzz gets wet I look
like a worm. Ugh!"
   "Don't be rude!" said the earthworm.

"Actually," the ant announced, "it's *not* raining. That girl is watering the seeds to make them grow."

When Gaily finished watering, she tried to
roll up the hose. By mistake, she got all
tangled up.

Later, a flock of birds flew into the garden. The earthworm was afraid of being eaten. He hid in the soil. But the sparrows ate only seeds.

   To frighten away the birds, Gaily and
Sebastian made a scarecrow that fluttered
in the breeze.
   The birds stayed away.

"Hooray! The radishes are up!" shouted Gaily
a few weeks later.

"But those are only green leaves," complained
Sebastian. "Where are the round, red parts?"

"The red parts are under the ground," said
Gaily, wisely. "They need more time to grow."

Later Gaily dug up a radish to see how big it was. The round, red part was too tiny to eat. Gaily put the radish back and packed the earth around it.

    As the vegetables grew, so did the weeds.
Some weeds were harder to pull out than others.
Once when Sebastian pulled one out, he toppled
over, just missing the earthworm, the snail,
the caterpillar, and the ant.

One day, Gaily discovered some little green bugs on the tomato plants. She went to her mother for advice.

"Those green bugs are called aphids," Gaily's mother said. "They are bad for plants."

"What a peculiar smell!" exclaimed the ant after Gaily and her mother had planted flowers called marigolds around the tomatoes.

The little green bugs didn't like the marigolds' smell. Soon the aphids were gone.

"Good riddance to bad rubbish," said the earthworm.

"How dare you!" replied the ant. "Some of my best friends are aphids."

The argument grew so fierce that they didn't notice anyone coming.

But Sebastian saw the stranger. He ran to Gaily. He shouted, "There's a tiger in your garden!"

Sebastian's family knew he sometimes made things sound bigger than they were. But the family was careful, just in case.

There was no tiger in the garden — just a large ginger cat.

Then came the day that Gaily picked many
kinds of delicious, fresh vegetables.

For a while, the earthworm rode on the
basket. Then Gaily saw him and put him on
the ground.

The earthworm wriggled back into the garden.

As he got there, Gaily and her family gave three cheers. The earthworm thought they were cheering for him, but they were really cheering for Gaily and her wonderful garden.

Hooray!